The Silver Swan

Michael Morpurgo

Illustrated by Christian Birmingham

PICTURE CORGI BOOKS

For Cyril George
in his first year
M.M.

To Ben
C.B.

A PICTURE CORGI BOOK : 978 0 552 54614 0

First published in Great Britain by Doubleday, a division of Random House Children's Publishers UK

PRINTING HISTORY
Doubleday edition published 2000
Picture Corgi edition published 2001

13

Text copyright © Michael Morpurgo 2000
Illustrations copyright © Christian Birmingham 2000

Designed by Ian Butterworth

The right of Michael Morpurgo to be identified as the author and of
Christian Birmingham as the illustrator of this work has been asserted in
accordance with the Copyright, Designs and Patents Act 1988

Picture Corgi Books are published by Random House Children's Publishers UK,
61-63 Uxbridge Road, London W5 5SA,
a division of The Random House Group Ltd,
Addresses for companies within The Random House Group Limited
can be found at : www.randomhouse.co.uk/offices.htm

Printed in China

www.randomhousechildrens.co.uk

The Silver Swan

The silver swan, who living had no note,
When death approached, unlocked her silent throat:
Leaning her breast against the reedy shore
Thus sung her first and last, and sung no more.

Orlando Gibbons

A swan came to my loch one day, a silver swan. I was fishing for trout in the moonlight. She came flying in above me, her wings singing in the air. She circled the loch twice, and then landed, silver, silver in the moonlight.

I stood and watched her as she arranged her wings behind her and sailed out over the loch making it entirely her own. I stayed as late as I could, quite unable to leave her.

I went down to the loch every day after that, but not to fish for trout, simply to watch my silver swan.

In those early days I took great care not to frighten her away, keeping myself still and hidden in the shadow of the alders. But even so, she knew I was there – I was sure of it.

Within a week I would find her cruising along the lochside, waiting for me when I arrived in the early mornings. I took to bringing some bread crusts with me. She would look sideways at them at first, rather disdainfully. Then, after a while, she reached out her neck, snatched them out of the water, and made off with them in triumph.

One day I dared to dunk the bread crusts for her, dared to try to feed her by hand. She took all I offered her and came back for more. She was coming close enough now for me to be able to touch her neck. I would talk to her as I stroked her. She really listened, I know she did.

I never saw the cob arrive. He was just there swimming beside her one morning out on the loch. You could see the love between them even then. The princess of the loch had found her prince. When they drank they dipped their necks together, as one. When they flew, their wings beat together, as one.

She knew I was there, I think, still watching. But she did not come to see me again, nor to have her bread crusts. I tried to be more glad for her than sad for me, but it was hard.

As winter tried, and failed, to turn to spring, they began to make a home on the small island, way out in the middle of the loch. I could watch them now only through my binoculars. I was there every day I could be – no matter what the weather.

Things were happening. They were no longer busy just preening themselves, or feeding, or simply gliding out over the loch taking their reflections with them. Between them they were building a nest – a clumsy messy excuse for a nest it seemed to me – set on a reedy knoll near the shore of their island.

It took them several days to construct. Neither ever seemed quite satisfied with the other's work. Either a twig was too big, or too small, or perhaps just not in the right place. There were no arguments as such, as far as I could see. But my silver swan would rearrange things, tactfully, when her cob wasn't there. And he would do the same, when she wasn't there.

Then, one bright cold morning with the ground beneath my feet hard with a late and unexpected frost, I arrived to see my silver swan enthroned at last on her nest, her cob proudly patrolling the loch close by.

I knew there were foxes about even then. I had heard their cries often enough echoing through the night. I had seen their footprints in the snow. But I had never seen one out and about, until now.

It was dusk. I was on my way back home from the loch, coming up through the woods, when I spotted a family of five cubs, their mother sitting on guard nearby. Unseen and unsmelt, I crouched down where I was and watched.

I could see at once that they were starving, some of them already too weak even to pester their mother for food. But I could see too that she had none to give – she was thin and rangy herself. I remember thinking then: that's one family of foxes that's not likely to make it, not if the spring doesn't come soon, not if this winter goes on much longer.

But the winter did go on that year, on and on.

I thought little more of the foxes. My mind was on other things, more important things. My silver swan and her cob shared the sitting duties and the guarding duties, never leaving the precious nest long enough for me even to catch sight of the eggs, let alone count them. But I could count the days, and I did.

As the day approached I made up my mind I would go down to the loch, no matter what, and stay there until it happened – however long that might take. But the great day dawned foggy. Out of my bedroom window, I could barely see across the farmyard.

I ran all the way down to the loch. From the lochside I could see nothing of the island, nothing of the loch, only a few feet of limpid grey water lapping at the muddy shore. I could hear the muffled *aarking* of a heron out in the fog, and the distant piping of a moorhen. But I stayed to keep watch, all that day, all the next.

I was there in the morning two days later when the fog began at last to lift and the pale sun to come through. The island was there again. I turned my binoculars at once on the nest. It was deserted. They were gone. I scanned the loch, still mist-covered in places. Not a ripple. Nothing.

Then out of nothing they appeared, my silver swan, her cob and four cygnets, coming straight towards me. As they came towards the shore they turned and sailed right past me. I swear she was showing them to me, parading them. They both swam with such easy power, the cygnets bobbing along in their wake. But I had counted wrong. There was another one, hitching a ride in amongst his mother's folded wings. A snug little swan, I thought, littler than the others perhaps. A lucky little swan.

That night the wind came in from the north and the loch froze over. It stayed frozen. I wondered how they would manage. But I need not have worried. They swam about, keeping a pool of water near the island clear of ice. They had enough to eat, enough to drink. They would be fine. And every day the cygnets were growing. It was clear now that one of them was indeed much smaller, much weaker. But he was keeping up. He was coping. All was well.

Then, silently, as I slept one night, it snowed outside. It snowed on the farm, on the trees, on the frozen loch. I took bread crusts with me the next morning, just in case, and hurried down to the loch. As I came out of the wood I saw the fox's paw-prints in the snow. They were leading down towards the loch.

I was running, stumbling through the drifts, dreading all along what I might find.

The fox was stalking around the nest. My silver swan was standing her ground over her young, neck lowered in attack, her wings beating the air frantically, furiously. I shouted. I screamed. But I was too late and too far away to help.

Quick as a flash the fox darted in, had her by the wing and was dragging her away. I ran out onto the ice. I felt it crack and give suddenly beneath me. I was knee-deep in the loch then, still screaming; but the fox would not be put off. I could see the blood, red, bright red on the snow. The five cygnets were scattering in their terror. My silver swan was still fighting. But she was losing, and there was nothing I could do.

I heard the sudden singing of wings above me. The cob! The cob flying in, diving to attack. The fox took one look upwards, released her victim, and scampered off over the ice, chased all the way by the cob.

For some moments I thought my silver
swan was dead. She lay so still on the
snow. But then she was on her feet and
limping back to her island, one wing
flapping feebly, the other trailing, covered
in blood and useless. She was gathering
her cygnets about her. They were all
there. She was enfolding them, loving
them, when the cob came flying back to
her, landing awkwardly on the ice.

He stood over her all that day and
would not leave her side. He knew she was
dying. So, by then, did I. I had nothing
but revenge and murder in my heart.
Time and again, as I sat there at the
lochside, I thought of taking my father's
gun and going into the woods to hunt
down the killer fox. But then I would
think of her cubs and would know that
she was only doing what a mother fox had
to do.

For days I kept my cold sad vigil by
the loch. The cob was sheltering the
cygnets now, my silver swan sleeping
nearby, her head tucked under her wing.
She scarcely ever moved.

I wasn't there, but I knew the precise moment she died. I knew it because she sang it. It's quite true what they say about swans singing only when they die. I was at home. I had been sent out to fetch logs for the fire before I went up to bed. The world about me was crisp and bright under the moon. The song was clearer and sweeter than any human voice, than any bird song, I had ever heard before. So sang my silver swan and died.

I expected to see her lying dead on the island the next morning. But she was not there. The cob was sitting still as a statue on his nest, his five cygnets around him.

I went looking for her. I picked up the trail of feathers and blood at the lochside, and followed where I knew it must lead, up through the wood. I approached silently. The fox cubs were frolicking fat and furry in the sunshine, their mother close by intent on her grooming. There was a terrible wreath of white feathers nearby, and telltale feathers too on her snout. She was trying to shake them off. How I hated her.

I ran at her. I picked up stones. I hurled them. I screamed at her. The foxes vanished into the undergrowth and left me alone in the woods. I picked up a silver feather, and cried tears of such raw grief, such fierce anger.

Spring came at long last the next day, and melted the ice. The cob and his five cygnets were safe. After that I came less and less to the loch. It wasn't quite the same without my silver swan. I went there only now and again, just to see how he was doing, how they were all doing.

At first, to my great relief, it seemed as if he was managing well enough on his own. Then one day I noticed there were only four cygnets swimming alongside him, the four bigger ones. I don't know what happened to the smaller one. He just wasn't there. Not so lucky, after all.

The cob would sometimes bring his cygnets to the lochside to see me. I would feed them when he came, but then after a while he just stopped coming.

The weeks passed and the months passed, and the cygnets grew and flew. The cob scarcely left his island now. He stayed on the very spot I had last seen my silver swan. He did not swim, he did not feed, he did not preen himself. Day by day it became clearer that he was pining for her, dying for her.

Now my vigil at the lochside was almost constant again. I had to be with him, to see him through. It was what my silver swan would have wanted, I thought.

So I was there when it happened. A swan flew in from nowhere one day, down onto the glassy stillness of the loch. She landed right in front of him. He walked down into the loch, settled into the water and swam out to meet her. I watched them look each other over for just a few minutes. When they drank, they dipped their necks together, as one. When they flew, their wings beat together, as one.

Five years on and they're still
together. Five years on and I still
have the feather from my silver swan.
I take it with me wherever I go.
I always will.